BOB ASHER

BOB ASHER

First Edition 2024

This is a story of fiction. The names, characters, organizations, places, events, and incidents are either products of my imagination or are used fictitiously.

Books by Bob Asher
Jon Smith Military/Espionage Thrillers
BEAR TRAP
ESCAPE FROM DONETSK
FLASH OVERRIDE (Coming soon)
CHRISTMAS REDEMPTION

Zack Goodson Crime Thrillers
HOPE IS DEAD

Once again, thank you, Sierra Kilo, for your patience and unwavering support while I locked myself up in my office at night to write this story.

Please join my newsletter using the link below for updates on future Jon Smith novels and short stories. I promise I won't sell or share your email address with anyone.
Bob Asher Books Newsletter

ISBN-13: 978-1-958115-08-4 (Paperback)
ISBN-13: 978-1-958115-09-1 (Hardcover)

Book Cover Design and Interior Formatting by 100Covers.

CHAPTER 1

0300, JULY 15, DAY 1,
35,000 FEET NEAR SINABANG,
SUMATRA ISLAND, ACEH, INDONESIA

Lightning jumped laterally from cloud to cloud. "What happened?" Kong asked over the secure UHF radio. Lieutenant Commander Steve "Kong" King was a test pilot with the United States Navy's Air Test and Evaluation Squadron Nine (VX-9).

"The missile didn't come off the rail. I think I took a lightning strike. Come over and take a look," Lieutenant Commander Tom "Spike" Jones replied. The missile was an experimental extended-range

AIM-174B air-to-air missile and a variant of the Navy's RIM-174 or Standard Missile 6 (SM-6) ship-launched missile. The AIM-174B air-to-air missile was the Navy's counter to China's hyper-sonic aircraft carrier killing missiles. It could fly at Mach 3.5 and intercept the Chinese shipkillers before they even got close. Spike and Kong were off the coast of Sumatra, one of the thousands of islands that made up the Republic of Indonesia, demonstrating the missile for America's ally, Australia.

Kong slid his F/A-18E Super Hornet fighter jet under Spike's Hornet. He looked up through his canopy to study the missile and the rail on the right wing it was attached to from a mere ten feet away. "I don't see any damage," Kong transmitted to Spike as he slid back to the right to give Spike room to maneuver.

"Well, I can't jettison it. I'll have to bring it back," Spike replied. The AIM-174B was still classified. He couldn't let the Chinese fish it out of the ocean. "Coming right," Spike transmitted. Kong remained in formation inside Spike's turn. Seconds later, still in the turn, Spike felt a thump. "What was that?" he asked.

Kong rolled inverted and dove for the cloud deck 10,000 feet below. "The missile fell off your rail. I'm chasing it. He formed up on the free-falling missile fifty feet from its tail just before it punched into the clouds. His eyes darted back and forth from the missile to the altitude indicated on his heads-up display or HUD. The clouds became broken at 9,000 feet above sea level and the missile stabilized at its terminal velocity of 520 knots. Kong throttled back to let the missile fall away and pressed target store on his navigation system before pulling out of his dive. He watched as the AIM-174B disappeared harmlessly into the thick jungle canopy covering the mountains of northern Sumatra. *Damn! That's going to be a problem!* Kong thought as he pulled out of his dive and turned back out to sea to form up on Spike. He looked at the lat long location on his NAV system and wrote it down on his kneeboard. He had inadvertently violated Indonesian air space.

CHAPTER 2

A white Lockheed L-100 freighter, the civilian variant of the mighty C-130 Hercules turboprop plane, from a Polish air cargo carrier passed low over the narrow beach and perimeter road before touching down on the numbers of Runway 07 at Lasikin Airport, in Sinabang, Indonesia. It raced past the midfield taxiway before the pilot could reverse the props in beta, so he continued to the end of Runway 25 to turn around. The Polish loadmaster walked over to where Jon Smith was sleeping on the red nylon bench seat and lightly kicked his boot. Jon sat up quickly, rubbing the sleep from his eyes. The cargo area was bathed in dim red light to preserve their night vision.

"We are arrived, Cowboy!" he shouted in broken English over the roar of the four massive turboprop engines.

Jon nodded and turned on the blue LED light hanging from his neck on 550 paracord. He scanned the area around him to ensure nothing fell out of his pockets or rucksack. He grabbed his Ops-Core high-cut ballistic helmet's straps and threw it onto his head. His four-banger ground panoramic night vision goggles were attached but stowed up out of his way until needed. He stood up and stretched his legs and back before shrugging on his one-hun-dred-pound pack. He stumbled back a step as the weight caught him off balance. He connected his HK416 rifle to his single-point sling before walk-ing over to the ramp to wait for the loadmaster to lower it. The Poles had briefed him that they would stop for one second just before they turned off the runway onto the midfield taxiway. That would be his signal to leave the plane. Seconds later the loadmaster grabbed the ramp lever and opened the ramp to only four inches above the asphalt.

Jon walked down to within a foot from the edge of the ramp to be ready to step off. Instead of slowly rolling to a gentle stop, the pilot stomped on the brake pedals causing the plane to lurch to a stop and Jon to fall backwards. "What the fuck, dammit!" Jon shouted at the loadmaster. Only his thick rucksack saved him from smacking his helmeted head on the ramp. He flailed his arms and legs like a giant sea turtle for a moment. "Help me up!" he yelled. The plane resumed rolling and rather than try any further to get up he rotated ninety degrees and rolled off the ramp. He stopped tumbling after a few revolutions and looked back at the loadmaster. He had his hands on his knees, obviously laughing his ass off. "Asshole!" Jon shouted, his angry outburst swallowed up by the loud engines and propellers. "And so it begins," Jon said to himself as he looked up at the stars. This mission sucked before it started, and he feared it would just get worse.

Jon staggered to his feet under his overloaded ruck. He lowered his NVGs and checked to make sure the ACOG optics and laser on his rifle weren't damaged. He felt for the suppressor in a chest rig compartment before he walked off across the grass to a small unused ramp 375 meters away. In the distance, he could see the pilot smoking as he stood next to his Cessna U206 airplane. *I guess he doesn't know smoking is bad for his night vision,* Jon thought. Jon covered the distance in a little over four minutes. He stopped about ten feet from the pilot who was wearing a Hawaiian shirt, cargo shorts, and Crocs. He said, "Good evening."

The pilot jumped back and dropped his cigarette as he shouted "Fuuuck! You scared the shit out of me!" His head scanned back and forth but he couldn't see Jon.

"My name is Jon," he said.

"Uh, yeah, okay. Good to meet you, Jon. You can call me, ah, Starlord," he said, his bright green teeth shining forth through Jon's NVGs.

"I was expecting a Night Stalker MH-60," Jon said only half joking as he looked at the small airplane.

"Yeah, they chickened out at the last minute, so the Agency called me," the pilot replied.

Jon walked past the man and said, "Well, okay then, Starlord." He dropped his rucksack into the plane through the large open cargo hatch on the right side of the plane behind the wing. It wasn't the worst nom de guerre he had ever heard. "Is that an alias?" Jon asked.

"No, it's my callsign from my Navy days," he replied.

"Oh yeah, aviator? What'd you fly?" Jon was pleased. Naval Aviators were always shit hot. Even at night in shitty weather, they were rock solid. He made the mistake of calling one of them a pilot once in the officer's club. The guy set him straight. *'Whoa, whoa, whoa, sonny. Pilots drive tugboats. Naval Aviators fly aerial instruments of war'* he said proudly.

"Super Hornets," Starlord said proudly.

"You're what, thirty? Why'd you get out?" Jon was curious.

"I had a ramp strike. Totaled my jet. They checked my vision and said some bullshit about my depth perception being a little off, so they grounded me," he explained. "But, hey, it's cool.

The Company's always looking for contract pilots. Don't worry, Jon. We won't be landing on any carriers tonight," he said before laughing.

Jon waited for the laughing to subside. "Okay. Where'd you get this parachute?" Jon asked as he pulled a RAM air parachute out of the cargo area.

"Pretty sweet, uh? It came from the 24th STS paraloft," Starlord replied. The USAF 24th Special Tactics Squadron was the only tier-one special operations unit in the Air Force.

"Why aren't they handling this mission? Retrieving people and shit is their primary mission," Jon said.

"I think they don't want to get caught operating in another country without their prior approval," Starlord explained.

"They'd probably think differently if it was an Air Force missile," Jon replied. Starlord nodded his agreement. *So, I guess I'm expendable. Why send the Night Stalkers and the D-boys when Jon's available,* Jon thought. "Fuck it. Let's go," he said in exasperation.

"Hop in. I'll get us started and over to Sumatra," Starlord said. Lasikin Airport was on Simeulue Island, about seventy miles off the coast of the much larger Sumatra Island where Jon was to remove a component from the target and destroy the rest.

The pilot fastened his seat belt before putting his green tiger-striped Gentex HGU-55/P fixed-wing helmet on. He had AN/AVS-9 NVGs mounted to his helmet. He lowered them before scanning the area to make sure no one was close by. "Clear," he said softly mostly out of habit. He didn't really want anyone to hear him. He cranked the engine and the prop immediately spun to life. "Close the cargo hatch, Jon," he said over the intercom system. "Are you set in back?" he asked.

Jon keyed his microphone twice to indicate affirmative.

"Okay, we're rolling," Starlord replied. He stopped at the near-invisible hold short markings before the runway. Normally, that would be where a pilot would call for permission to takeoff, but the tower controllers didn't see him sneak in to land an hour and a half earlier with his lights off and now they wouldn't see him when he snuck out of the airport. Starlord looked both ways through his NVGs and seeing no traffic nor hearing any on the radio, he fire-walled his throttle as he turned left onto Runway 25 and took off against the wind. He cleared the fence and beach at 100 feet before entering a gentle right turn to the northeast and climbing up to 900 feet to stay at least 100 feet above ground level. As they went feet wet on the east side of Simeulue Island, Starlord climbed to three hundred feet above the water and set the throttle to maintain 140 knots. After a few minutes, Starlord's secure tablet lit up. He read it quickly and handed it back to Jon. "Here's an update on your mission."

Jon read the information quietly to himself, *Location of target confirmed at 3.7333°, 97.1956°. NSA advised Chinese MSS aware of the nature of your target. They have dispatched a team to recover it intact for evaluation. ETA unknown.* MSS was The Ministry of State Security or MSS. It was China's equivalent of the CIA, except much more sinister. He tried to scroll down on the message but that's all there was. Jon dropped the tablet over the seat back next to the pilot. "Where's the rest of the message where they say to abort because you're outnumbered and outgunned?" Jon asked, clearly dismayed.

"I guess the target's too important to let the Chinese get a hold of it," Starlord stated the obvious. "No worries, I'll drop you on a patch of cleared land uphill from the jungle where the target is. That way you can do your thing and di di mau down the mountain to the PZ." Seconds later he said, "We'll be over the drop zone in another twenty minutes."

Resigned to his fate, Jon put on his parachute and connected his rucksack to his parachute harness so he wouldn't lose it. He put on his clear eye pro and waited. His mind raced with a constant flow of what could go wrong. Despite serving twenty years as a Navy SEAL before retiring to join the Agency's Special Activities Division, he never learned to enjoy skydiving. He had hundreds of jumps, and he was an expert, but he hated every one of them.

"Three minutes, Jon," Starlord warned over the ICS, "Hey, why don't we exchange numbers just in case you run into any problems? I should be able to get to you within three or four hours and my rates are a lot cheaper than JSOC's."

CHAPTER 3

Senior MSS Officer Su Chin stood before his eleven-man team in the MSS Field Office conference room in Medan. "Comrades, the Chairman has entrusted us with a vital mission for the People. Our Indonesian friends have informed us the American Imperialist Navy violated Indonesian airspace and dropped an experimental weapon in a remote area of the Gunung Leuser National Park. We believe the weapon is a long-range air-to-air missile capable of intercepting our DF-21 hypersonic anti-ship ballistic missiles. This weapon is an existential threat to our national defense. He pointed to a map displayed on the large TV mounted on the wall. "We believe the missile fell in this area, sixteen kilometers south of Mount Leuser," he said.

"Sir, have the Americans sent a recovery team to retrieve the missile?" Officer Chen Qui, Su's second in command asked.

"Good question, Chen. We don't know but we must assume they have," Su replied.

"What are our rules of engagement?" Chen asked.

"Deadly force is authorized and most likely expected. We must seize this missile at all costs," Su explained. Su took a moment to look around the room at his men. He was impressed by every one of them. "If there are no more questions grab your equipment and head to the helicopter," he said.

CHAPTER 4

0030, JULY 17, DAY 3,
DROP ZONE, GUNUNG LEUSER NATIONAL PARK,
SUMATRA ISLAND, NORTH SUMATRA, INDONESIA

Jon checked his GPS to confirm the location before grabbing the bottom of the fiberglass door and sliding it up out of the way. He leaned out to make sure they were over land. The jungle-covered mountains in the Gunung Leuser National Park climbed to as high as 11,000 feet. Jon would be jumping about ten miles south of Mount Leuser where the elevation was only 6,000 feet. He lowered his GPNVGs over his eyes and sat in the opening with his legs dangling. Starlord tapped his shoulder and Jon leaned forward, exiting the airplane.

Jon deployed his chute immediately and turned it toward his landing zone. He flew his canopy down in a wide circle over his landing spot. As he approached the rocky mountainside a gust of wind came over the crest and rushed down on Jon, depleting the lift in his RAM airfoil and dropping him toward the trees short of the LZ. Jon looked between his legs as the trees rushed up to him. *This is going to hurt!* he thought. He quickly released his rucksack to dangle fifteen feet below between his legs. He crossed his legs and let go of the parachute risers to cover his face. He pinballed down through the trees with his legs and arms bouncing off large branches and trunks. His canopy snagged above him, and he came to a halt twenty-five feet in the air. "Oooooh," he moaned softly.

He just hung there silently with his eyes closed, slowly taking inventory of his limbs and what hurt where. Finally, he concluded he hurt all over. He opened his eyes and discovered his GPNVGs had been knocked loose from their mount and were dangling in front of him on their lanyard. He snapped them back into their mount and surveyed his surroundings. On his right, he saw only dense jungle. He turned back to the left and immediately recoiled as he saw the face of a giant green orangutan looking back at him. It bared its teeth in what Jon hoped was a smile. Jon slowly reached into his right cargo pocket and retrieved a bag of Skittles candy he had ratfucked from an MRE. Jon tore the bag open and offered it to the giant ape. The orangutan accepted the bag and slowly sniffed it before putting the bag in his mouth. He chewed briefly, swallowed, and smiled again. Jon reached back into the pocket and pulled out his only Snicker's bar. He peeled the wrapper and handed it over. He hoped it would keep the ape chewing until he could get out of the tree.

Jon's rucksack was dangling fifteen feet below him on a nylon strap. He released it, letting it fall through the branches. He pulled another nylon strap from his chest pocket and snapped it to the D-ring on his chest before lowering himself to the ground. He wrestled his rucksack onto his back and checked his GPS before slowly making his way downhill through the heavy brush.

CHAPTER 5

Jon Smith was making relatively good time considering he was humping through the darkened jungle surrounded by creatures and terrain that wanted to kill him. *At least I'm going downhill,* he thought. He was constantly checking his GPS. As he took a step, he heard something to his left. He turned to look, causing his right foot to slip on the detritus of thousands of years of rotting foliage. He slid off the game trail and tumbled into a ravine, coming to a stop fifty feet further down the hill with the wind knocked out of him. He gasped for air until the feeling subsided. He seriously wondered what creepy crawlies were climbing around on and under his clothes. He had taken one precaution. He was wearing a pair of nylon pantyhose. He had been taught early on in his career that SEALs in the Vietnam War wore them to keep leeches from attaching to their legs and nether regions. Jon always defaulted to, 'If it works, it's not stupid.'

Jon took a moment while he was sitting to get a drink of water from his CamelBak. He heard something breathing to his left. He slowly turned his head to the left as he moved his right hand toward his Glock 21SF pistol. A huge orangutan sat on his haunches an arm's length away watching him. *No way. He can't be the same orangutan,* he thought. The orangutan shot him a huge green toothy smile and held his hand out. *Son of a bitch! It is him!* he thought. Jon reached into his pocket to retrieve a small bag of Starburst jellybeans. He opened the bag and poured a few into his palm and held it out for his companion. *Please, don't bite my hand off,* he thought. The giant mooch popped them in his mouth and chewed. The ape smiled appreciatively before placing his hand on Jon's shoulder and then pointing behind Jon back up the hill. Jon stood up and turned to scan the area through his GPNVGs. Through a break in the trees, he saw a train of human-shaped green blobs moving down the trail two hundred meters above him. "Thanks, buddy," Jon said quietly before handing him the bag of jellybeans. He turned and hurried down the hill angling to the left through the dense brush.

***

Two hours later, MSS Senior Officer Su Chin and four of his men arrived at the point on the animal trail where Jon had tumbled into the ravine. They were wearing Chinese third-generation night vision goggles. They were clones of the Thales LUCIE NVGs, a popular European NVG. Most importantly, they were inferior to the GPNVGs Jon was using. Earlier an unarmed drone had observed Jon parachuting into the mountain but had been unable to track him through the dense triple-canopy jungle. Su and his men had been able to locate Jon's parachute and track him to this point. Now they searched the ground for any sign indicating which direction Jon had taken.

A grunt to their right startled the men. Several brought their weapons up to fire, but Officer Su shouted, "No! You will give away our position." A fuzzy green orangutan sat on the trunk of a fallen tree. He smiled at the men with his hand out like a common Beijing street beggar. Su stepped forward to get between his men and the ape. The green giant motioned again with his hand, palm up. Su retrieved a spring onion cracker from his pocket and gave it to the ape. He put it in his mouth and chewed it up eagerly but soon his expression changed as he scraped his tongue against his teeth trying to get the unappetizing taste out of his mouth. He smiled and pointed down the hill to the right, away from Jon's path.

Officer Su bowed to the orangutan in thanks and said, "Follow me," to his men before leading them down the hill in the wrong direction.

CHAPTER 6

**0616, JULY 17, DAY 3,
AIM-174B MISSILE CRASH SITE,
GUNUNG LEUSER NATIONAL PARK**

Jon followed his GPS as he meandered down the mountain. It was almost time for the sun to rise. The sky had lightened enough for him to stow his GPNVGs in his pack. Minutes later, he arrived at the target's lat long and looked around. Nothing. He began searching in ever-widening circles. After five minutes he was fifty feet down the hill. Fifteen feet to his right he saw a boulder jutting five feet out of the ground. Gray paint had been transferred onto the jagged rock. Fifty feet further down the hill he found the missile bent but intact, well hidden by the trees.

Jon shrugged off his pack and retrieved the toolkit he had been briefed on using. *Where is it?* he thought as he looked. *Please, don't be underneath,* he prayed. After a few seconds, he located the correct access panel and opened it with his cordless screwdriver. He reached inside the missile and wrestled with the components. *C'mon, let go, dammit.* Finally, he was able to free the missile's brain. He stuffed it in his cargo pocket. He stopped and looked around in all directions. He felt very lonely, one man against China. Next, he reached into his pack for two satchel charges. The M183 Demolition Charge Assemblies contained twenty pounds of C-4 explosives in each satchel. Jon quickly placed the charges on the missile and attached a remote radio detonator receiver to both satchel charges. Jon quickly closed his pack and threw it over his shoulders, now at least forty pounds lighter.

He rushed away into the jungle far enough to feel safe and stopped under cover to check his GPS. He pulled out his encrypted satellite telephone and typed a message, Package located, item recovered, charges set. Ready for pick up. A response came back instantly, exfil at primary PZ at 0705. Jon studied his GPS map display and found a piece of high ground between his current location and the PZ within two miles of the missile. He wanted to ensure he would have a line of sight with the missile so his MK152, remote radio detonator would work. It was normally good for three miles.

Jon made his way across the mountainside under the jungle canopy. He found a rocky shelf under the trees that provided an excellent view of the missile's location. He shed his pack and laid down on the shelf to scope the area with his ACOG. He glimpsed five men walking off the trail. "Shit!" he said to himself as he reached for his detonator. He had to blow the charges before they had time to disable the detonators. He armed the transmitter and pressed the button. Instantly, flaming trees flew into the air in all directions before an orange and black fireball boiled up into the sky. A split second later he heard the explosion roll across the terrain. He crawled backward off the shelf, dragging his rucksack with him. Once on his feet, he shouldered his pack and headed off to the PZ. He checked his GPS and realized he would have to hurry.

***

"Streetwalker, this is Wombat 22," the Australian Army helicopter's copilot transmitted over his secure radio.

"Go for Streetwalker," Jon replied out of breath as he hurried toward the pick-up zone. *Where do they get these stupid call signs? He was a retired SEAL for crying out loud. He should be called Neptune or Hammerhead, something cool.*

"We are five mikes out, mate. Don't be late. We can't hover about," the pilot transmitted.

"No worries. I'll put the tea on for you," Jon said as he cranked it up a notch. He could rest when he was dead. Jon gave up any pretense of trying to be stealthy as he crashed through the brush with his Garmin GPS in one hand and his machete in the other. He arrived at the edge of the clearing just in time to hear the helo approaching. He could tell it was a Black Hawk from the sound. *Thank God! At least this time they sent the varsity to get me,* he thought. He half expected a little Robinson R-22 helicopter. With two seats, they were great for taking flying lessons on weekends or flying cross country some- where for a $400 hamburger. Then he realized, *the Black Hawk's not for me, it's for the missile's computer brain. If I had failed to retrieve it, they would have made me walk to the coast and swim out to sea to be picked up.*

CHAPTER 7

"We'll be over the PZ in one minute," the copilot announced over the ICS. The 171st Special Operations Aviation Squadron's S-70A Black Hawk helicopter had a four-man crew, two were pilots and two were door gunners.

Four Australian SASR operators were also on board. Three of them were new to the Regiment, fresh out of training. They were led by a crusty veteran who had been in the SASR for twelve years. They were there to help retrieve Jon and were heavily armed in case the helicopter ran into any trouble. They were highly skilled and supremely confident in their abilities.

"Angie, who's this yank we're picking up?" The youngest, Caleb asked.

"Just another arrogant American super soldier, here to show us what's what. No worries, you don't have to introduce him to your kid sister. We'll just pick him up and RTB," Angie replied.

Just as the helicopter flared to land in a small rocky clearing, a tiny missile streaked over the jungle canopy from two kilometers away. "Missile, ten o'clock!" the copilot yelled into the ICS. The pilot slid to the right causing the MANPAD to miss the cockpit and zoom under the rotor blades before exploding into the tail rotor.

Despite stomping on the left anti-torque pedal, the helicopter ignored the pilot and immediately spun out of control. He shouted, "We're going down!" as the helicopter began spinning ever faster. The SASR soldiers were flung helplessly from the open cabin doors. The pilot lowered the collective quickly to reduce the spinning which resulted in the helicopter landing hard and bouncing onto its side, shattering its rotor blades. Fortunately, the pilots had crash-worthy, armored seats that could withstand a 16G impact. Unfortunately, the seat provided no help when it came to fire suppression. The self-sealing fuel tank failed, spewing fuel into the cabin and cockpit which quickly erupted into a white-hot furnace. The helicopter was engulfed in acrid black smoke and angry orange flames.

***

Jon turned away to protect his eyes from flying debris generated by the helo's rotor downwash. He heard the missile's explosion and looked up in time to see the helicopter spin out of control and eject its passengers before crashing. "Oh my God!" Jon shouted, instantly aware that good men he had never met were dying for him. He sprinted out of the brush on the edge of the clearing and ran to the burning Black Hawk that had rolled over on its right side. Jon got as close as he could to see the pilots. They were moving but already burned beyond recognition. He couldn't see inside the cabin, but it was fully engulfed. The only sounds came from the flames dancing out of the cargo compartment. Jon heard screams and turned to see a burning soldier rolling back and forth on the ground. He was on fire from head to toe.

The man screamed long and loud in agony before shouting, "Angie! Help me! Help me, please!"

Jon rushed toward the soldier on the edge of the clearing but hearing a deafening rifle shot from behind him, he skidded to a stop as the soldier's head burst open in front of him. Jon turned to face the gunman. It was another Aussie SAS man thirty meters away. His right leg was bent at an unnatural angle below his knee. He held his rifle with his right hand and rested the forearm on his raised left knee. His bloody left arm rested limp at his side. Jon walked cautiously over to the man, careful to keep his muzzle down and away from him. "Sorry about your man. I was trying to help him," Jon said as he took a knee in front of the soldier.

"No worries, mate. I gave him what he was asking for. He would've done the same for me," the soldier replied stoically.

"I'm Jon, what's your name?"

"Hawkins," he replied before wincing in pain.

"Do you have anything I can give you for the pain?" Jon asked.

"I already took some fentanyl citrate. It'll kick in soon. I don't want any more until we sort out our next move," he replied.

"Yeah, fentanyl's good but morphine's always been my favorite," Jon replied, before looking back over his shoulder. "I better go check on your other men."

"Don't bother," Hawkins said as he pointed. "Nigel, over there, landed on his head and Clive shot himself after realizing his back was broken. How much time do you think we have before they get to us?"

"Yeah, about that. Here's the thing, Hawkins. I killed a handful of these little ChiCom bastards before I called for the helo. I don't know how many more of them are going to come running down the mountain but I'm sure they're coming. That missile I blew up is a game-changer. Once operational it could keep China from invading Taiwan. If they don't take Taiwan in the next few years they never will. Don't worry, I'm going to get you off this mountain, but I can't outrun these assholes with you on my back. So, you're going to have to stay here for a while and I'll hide on the other side of the LZ and ambush them when they come over here to interrogate you," Jon explained.

"Hold on a damn minute, mate! What if they decide to skip the talk and shoot me in the head from a distance?" Hawkins asked.

"Naw, they won't do that. I destroyed the missile before they could get their grubby little hands on it, so they'll want something important to bring home to make up for their failure. We need to put them on their heels. Trust me, bro. I got this," Jon said before he turned and disappeared into the jungle.

***

"Wait!" was all Hawkins got out before Jon vanished into the smoke from the burning helicopter. *You better not be legging it,* he thought. Soon, he heard the Chinese stomping through the bush like a herd of elephants. They were excited after downing the chopper. He had two choices. He could go out in a blaze of glory or play dead. He opted for the latter, slumping his head forward and letting his hand drop out of his rifle's grip. *This plan better work,* Hawkins worried to himself.

Minutes later he heard shouts coming from the brush on the far side of the PZ. He hid his pistol and holster in the tall grass next to his right hand. Next, he flipped the safety off his rifle before quickly returning his hand to his lap. Either way, this should all be over soon. He waited and watched. All he saw in front of him was the burning helicopter and swirling black smoke. The Chinese must have shut up after they found the clearing. As if on cue, they emerged at the same time through the smoke, two on the left and three to the right. They approached him cautiously with their rifles up. *Where are you, Jon?* Angie thought.

Two men stopped fifteen feet in front of him. The one on the left said something in Chinese and the other man moved forward and took Hawkin's rifle. He stepped back next to his leader and dropped the rifle on the ground. The leader turned to the other three and said something. They immediately turned and disappeared to the other side of the burning helicopter.

"Who are you?" the man asked in thickly accented English.

Hawkins remained silent. He heard the foreign snap of a suppressor intermixed with the crackling fire from the burning flesh and helicopter. Then he heard it twice more. The Chinese leader also heard the sound and turned his head. He shouted an order to his last man. The man turned and cautiously approached the black curtain with his rifle up ready to fire. He disappeared into the black. Seconds later he screamed before stumbling back into view with a machete stuck deep into his body between his neck and severed collarbone. He fell to his knees and collapsed at his leader's feet. The leader, now terrified, raised his automatic rifle and began firing into the smoke.

Hawkins retrieved his pistol from the grass and shot the leader in the back of his head. The five-meter shot was easy for this highly trained warrior. "Streetwalker! Are you alright?" Hawkins shouted. "Are you alright, mate?"

"Give me a minute!" Jon shouted back. Shortly he reappeared through the smoke rubbing his chest under his armor. "I took a round in my plate," he replied, holding up a damaged thirty-round PMag. He put his boot on his last victim's shoulder and worked the machete back and forth until it came free. Next, he picked up Hawkins's rifle and gave it back to him before taking a knee. "How can I help you get ready to move?" Jon asked.

"I'm a medic and I have a kit in my pack. Get two splints, one for my leg and one for my arm," Hawkins said.

Jon dug them out and unrolled the first splint. It had a moldable aluminum plate in the center covered by closed cell foam on both sides.

"My tibia and fibula are broken. You need to straighten my leg and then put the splint on it. Make sure to mold the splint tight and tape it from top to bottom. Give me that PMag," Hawkins said. He stuck it in his mouth and nodded.

"Okay, here goes," Jon twisted Hawkins's right boot ninety degrees as he bit down on the maga-zine and grimaced. Jon quickly molded the splint to his leg and wrapped tape around it as fast as he could. Hawkins was panting in short rapid breaths. Slowly, he recovered and wiped tears from his eyes. "It's time for more fentanyl," he said as he fished another fentanyl citrate lozenge from his pocket.

Jon saw bite marks on the hard plastic magazine. He unrolled the other splint. "Where do you want this one?" he asked.

"I landed on my left arm. One or both of my radius and ulna are broken, and I buggered up my shoulder. Curve the splint around my hand and forearm and bend it at my elbow so we can put my arm in a sling," Hawkins replied.

"Do I need to twist your forearm like I did your leg?" Jon asked.

"No! Please, try not to twist it, mate," Hawkins replied as he put the PMag back in his mouth.

Jon worked as fast as he could molding the splint into shape on his arm and then wrapping it in tape. He retrieved an OD green sling from Hawkins's pack and carefully positioned his arm in it.

Hawkins removed the magazine from his mouth and said, "Thanks, mate. That should work for now."

"You're welcome and I'm sorry," Jon replied.

"What do you have to apologize for?" Hawkins asked in confusion.

"Your boys are dead, and you're busted up because you came here to get me," Jon replied, his voice cracking with emotion.

"I didn't know you from Adam until today but we're all soldiers doing the bidding of our nations. Everyone on the chopper volunteered and fought for the opportunity to be on this mission. No apologies are necessary or requested. If anything, we should celebrate their lives and be grateful that more of such men exist," Hawkins said.

Jon smiled back with tears in his eyes. He held his hand out and said, "Lieutenant Commander Jon Smith, US Navy, retired. Now SAD SOG."

Hawkins shook his hand and said, "Warrant Officer 1 Angus Hawkins, Australian SASR. Call me Angie."

"Pleased to meet you, Angie. Now back to business. We need to downsize our gear. Go through your pack and put what you absolutely need in my butt pack," Jon said as he unclipped his butt pack and placed it on the ground next to

Angie. He and Angie quickly began tossing gear into the small pack. Soon it was full, and Jon closed the lid and snapped it around his waist. "I think that's around twenty pounds. Okay, I'm going to come behind you and help you up on your good leg," Jon said as he wrapped his arms around Angie and lifted him up on his left foot. "Okay, here we go," Jon said as he took Angie's right wrist in his left hand and wrapped his right arm around Angie's right thigh before raising him off the ground into a fireman's carry. Jon turned and started down the slope through the brush. "Does your radio work?" Jon asked. "We need to report what happened and get them working on the alternate exfil plan."

Angie keyed his PTT button and transmitted, "Vanguard, this is Streetwalker. Do you copy?"

"Go ahead, Streetwalker," the young radio operator replied.

"Wombat 22 has been shot down by MAN-PAD. All aboard are KIA except Echo 1. Echo 1 has a broken right leg and left arm. Streetwalker is carrying Echo 1 away from the crash site, over," Angie transmitted.

"Vanguard copies all, standby," the radio operator replied.

"I'm going to keep heading downhill toward the beach. They're not going to risk another helo to bring us out. We'll have to steal a boat or swim out to sea to be picked up. Damn, I hate swimming, everything in the water is trying to kill you," Jon complained. "Keep an eye on our six. There's no telling how many ChiComs are looking for us."

"I'm afraid you're right, mate," Angie replied.

Five minutes later, Vanguard transmitted, "Streetwalker, this is Vanguard."

"Go ahead, sir," Angie replied. He knew he was talking to the mission commander, Brigadier General Sanford, this time.

"The risk is too high to send another helicopter. Move to the beach. ASDS will pick you up 500 meters out," Vanguard transmitted. The ASDS or Advanced SEAL Delivery System was a long-range submersible capable of delivering or retrieving special operations forces on clandestine missions.

"Streetwalker copies, out," Angie replied.

"That's the story of my life, Angie," Jon said as he maneuvered through the trip me, fuck me vines.

"And where do they get these stupid callsigns like Streetwalker?" Jon stopped and looked at a cute little tree dweller sitting on a branch just ten feet away. "That's a cute little, whatever it is," Jon said, "It looks like it's part monkey part meerkat."

"Yeah, they're cute alright," Angie replied. "It's called a Slow Loris. It's the only poisonous primate in the world. If it bites you it could lead to a long agonizing death.

***

An hour and a half had passed before Senior Officer Su Chin and his four teammates arrived at the site of the Wombat 22 shootdown. He had observed the missile strike from two kilometers away, but it had taken his team much longer than he expected to traverse the hilly jungle terrain. Fortunately, the black smoke continued to rise from the smoldering helicopter the entire time and showed them the way like a beacon. He stopped at the edge of the clearing and sent his men out ahead of him to make sure it was safe.

One of his underlings returned and bowed before saying, "Officer Su, the crash site is secure. All of the foreigners are dead. Most of them perished in the fire."

"Have you seen Officer Chen Qui?" Su asked.

"Yes, sir. He is dead on the far side of the clearing. This way, sir," Officer Hui Jing said. He pointed at three bodies on the ground and said, "These bodies are Officers Min, Wu, and Qing. They were shot in the face with a rifle." He pointed at another body before saying, "This is Officer Lim, sir. They tried to cut his head off."

"This man we are hunting is a barbarian," Su replied in disgust.

"Officer Chen is over here, sir," Hui said as he led him. "He was also shot in the back of the head." He pointed to the open rucksacks. "Sir, I believe two foreigners survived and consolidated their equipment because one of them cannot walk. We should be able to catch up to them if one is carrying the other."

"Very good, Hui. Have the helicopter fly a team to the coastline and then have it pick me up here. We will trap them between our forces. We must try to take them alive if we can. Take the rest of our team and follow them down the mountain. We need to finish this mission before the Indonesians become involved," Senior Officer Su said.

CHAPTER 8

Jon was making slow but steady progress as he carried Angie down the mountain. His legs, back, and shoulders were aching. They heard a helicopter fly over from East to West. Jon stopped and they looked up, but the jungle's canopy obscured the sky. "I guess they're sending people down to the coast to get ahead of us," Jon speculated.

"Yeah, that's what I'd do, mate," Angie replied. "Hey! What's that on the trail in front of us?" he asked.

Jon stepped forward and looked down. "It's blood and entrails from something," he said.

"See that brown fur? That's from a Muntjac deer," Angie said softly.

"What's big enough to hunt the deer up here?" Jon asked.

"Sumatra Tigers are my best guess," Angie replied.

"Uh-uh! Nope! I don't do fucking tigers," Jon said nervously as he looked around as best he could with Angie on his shoulders.

"Relax, mate. Sumatra Tigers are about the smallest species of tiger, and they are very rare," Angie tried to comfort him.

"How small?" Jon asked in a whisper.

"The males are maybe eight feet long and around 300 pounds," Angie replied softly.

"Are you shitting me? Three hundred pounds of muscle, fangs, and claws isn't small," Jon said nervously as he flipped off the safety on his suppressed HK416.

"Jon, you can't shoot it," Angie whispered.

"Oh, I beg to differ," Jon replied.

"That 5.56mm round will just piss him off. If you empty your mag into him, he may die in a few hours, but it won't be in time to help us. Plus, even with the suppressor, the shots will be loud enough to flush all of the birds and monkeys out of the trees. That will give our position away if MSS is watching," Angie replied. "Let's just slowly edge around the entrails and make our way down the trail."

Jon did as instructed, using his right hand to point his rifle toward the left side of the trail where he believed the tiger had carried the deer carcass. As he worked his way slowly around the offal, he heard a low guttural growl that he felt pass completely through his chest to his spine. Every hair on his body stood at attention. His finger involuntarily crept closer to his trigger. He stepped back a foot to gain a bit of distance and his world was instantly upended. His left foot slipped in the mud and flew up in the air past his eyes followed quickly by his right. "Fuck!" he shouted as he landed hard on his back. The only thing available to cushion his fall was Angie's good left leg. They felt themselves falling off the trail, sliding head-first down a steep slope through a dark tunnel of low-hanging trees and lush green brush. They accelerated through the tunnel for another one hundred feet until they burst into the sunlight and saw themselves plunging another sixty feet through the air headfirst toward the rapidly flowing white water of an unknown river. Jon actually felt relieved to be falling toward the water. When in trouble, SEALs always went toward water. "Hang on to me, Angie!" Jon shouted, trying to sound confident.

"Crikey!" Angie yelled as they fell.

***

The tiger watched as he sat on all fours with his deer between his front legs. The humans kept coming closer. Finally, he growled to warn them off, but they made such a commotion as they were leaving, that he felt compelled to chase them. He launched himself across the trail and down the hill so fast he was sliding out of control before he realized what was happening. He flew into the open air head down. Seeing the water rushing up at him, he clawed at the air until he was upright.

***

"Hold your breath!" was all Jon could shout before they disappeared into the deep green water. Though it seemed like an eternity, Jon bobbed to the surface in four seconds. He treaded water as he was swept along in the rapids. He spun around looking for Angie just in time to see the falling tiger contorting himself before impacting the water feet first before sinking. "Oh, shit!"

The tiger surfaced, shook the water off his head, and began immediately dog paddling for Angie. With one good arm and leg, he was struggling to keep his head above water. Jon quickly swam thirty feet to place himself between Angie and the giant cat. Jon took a deep breath and submerged. He was confident he could hold his breath for at least two and a half minutes. Jon drew his Ka-Bar knife and waited. He maneuvered slightly to the left and held his right arm out with the seven-inch blade pointed up. As the tiger passed him, Jon thrust the blade up into the tiger's abdomen and grabbed his tail with his left hand. He quickly pulled the blade to the rear, opening a jagged nine-inch wound. The tiger instinctively brought his rear claws up to fight off whatever was biting him. The right claw dug a furrow across the top of Jon's right forearm forcing him to remove the blade and retreat. Jon submerged deeper to get away from the flailing claws.

The tiger turned back to face what had attacked him, losing interest in Angie. Jon swam under the cat and came up under and behind Angie into a lifeguard position to begin towing him away. A bloody pool formed around the big cat as it turned back toward Angie. "Jon, he's coming back!" Angie shouted as he kicked with his good leg. Jon was already gassed, but he increased his effort as much as he could. "Hurry!" Angie yelled in terror as the tiger closed to within several feet.

Jon turned to look just in time to see a massive saltwater crocodile's jaws rise from the water to clamp down on the tiger's neck and begin to thrash him about. The tiger howled loudly and clawed at the crocodile's head and snout as the crocodile rolled the tiger over and submerged with him never to be seen again. "Oh, my God! How big is that thing?" Jon shouted as he redoubled his efforts to kick and claw for the edge of the river. Angie had his pistol up above the water pointed to their rear just in case another monster appeared. Seconds later, Jon found his feet on semi-solid mud and slowly stood up as he dragged Angie to mostly dry land. He sat down next to Angie gasping for air as he tried to catch his breath. "I've never seen any-thing like that. The fucking tiger jumped off the mountain to chase us. He already had a kill. Why'd he come after us?" Jon asked.

"Beats me, mate. I'm gobsmacked," Angie said as he fished another fentanyl lozenge out of his pocket. He handed one to Jon, who gratefully unwrapped it.

"And that, croc. It was fucking massive," Jon said. "It had to be fifteen feet long."

Angie nodded his agreement. "The big ones get up around twenty."

"If one of those big son of a bitches comes our way, he's getting a lead enema," Jon said. He looked his rifle over to see if it would still function. "I'm surprised my rifle is still on its sling." They heard a soft grunt and jerked their heads around. Angie had his pistol up to shoot. "Hold up, Angie. It's okay. I met this mooch last night," Jon said as they looked at the big orangutan. "Do you have any candy? He has a sweet tooth," Jon said.

Angie pulled a brown MRE packet of grape jelly out of his pocket, "Here you go, mate," he said.

Jon tore the top open and handed it over, "Here you go, buddy." The ape smiled and sucked the jelly out of the pouch in one motion.

"Streetwalker, this is Vanguard, over," the radio operator transmitted over their secure radios.

"Go for Streetwalker," Jon replied.

"The Chinese Navy is patrolling off the West coast of Sumatra Island. We're unable to make the pick-up. You need to go to ground and standby until we come up with another plan, over," Vanguard transmitted.

"That's bullshit! Echo 1 does not have time for you to develop another plan! When we get out of the mountains you need to have assets standing by! Get Vanguard Actual on the radio now, mother-fucker!" Jon shouted into the radio. Vanguard actual was JSOC Brigadier General Edward Sanford.

"This is Vanguard Actual, over," General Sanford replied.

"Echo 1 needs a medivac ASAP! He doesn't have time for another plan to be worked up!" Jon explained rather loudly. He didn't care if the man was a fucking general.

"Streetwalker, we understand your situation and we are working the problem. Hunker down, son, and we'll get back to you," the general replied. Jon was fed up. He had known this asshole for ten years. He was one of those ass-kissing staff wee-nies who rose through the ranks without risking his own life in the field. He was only two years older than Jon.

"I'll give you fifteen seconds to clear the room, Sandy, before I lay things out for you," Jon transmitted.

"Just say your piece, Streetwalker, and then clear the net," Vanguard Actual replied.

"Sandy, if you leave us swinging in the wind, I'm going to break your nose and both of your arms! You won't be able to scratch your nose, wipe your ass, or jerk off for at least six weeks, out!" Jon shouted into his mic.

Angie busted out laughing. "Ow, dammit! Stop making me laugh!" Angie said, "Look! You scared off the moocher!" Angie pointed to the large ape who had moved off into the trees.

"Fuck that asshole. It's time for Plan B," Jon said before he dialed a number on his sat phone, mildly surprised that it still worked.

"Hello," the distant voice said.

"Hey, Starlord, this is Streetwalker," Jon said.

"What's up, buddy? I'm hanging out by the pool, working on my tan. Why don't you c'mon over?" Starlord asked. He was chilling next to the Officer's Club pool at Paya Lebar Air Base in Singapore.

"I need immediate pick up on the West coast of Sumatra downhill from where you dropped me. I have a friend with a broken arm and leg and unknown internal injuries," Jon explained.

Starlord put down his frou-frou umbrella drink and sat up in his lounge chair. "I thought you had pick-up already arranged," he said.

"The ChiComs shot down the helo and now the boys from Tampa are having cold feet. My boss will pay for this lift, three times your normal rate but I need you ASAP," Jon replied.

"It's going to take me three to four hours to get there. Standby for a second while I check my map." A moment later, he said, "Copy this lat long, 3.725°, 96.8367°."

Jon had the map feature open on his ATAK-MIL-equipped phone and said unsure, "That's a road, not a runway." ATAK stood for Android Team Awareness Kit.

"There are no runways where you're heading," Starlord replied as he was hurrying toward the shower room. "If I don't hear from you, I'm going to land and wait for five minutes. If you don't show or I start getting shot at I'll leave."

"Understood. Thanks, brother, out," Jon said before stuffing the phone back in his pocket.

CHAPTER 9

**1020, JULY 17, DAY 3,
LABUHANHAJI,
SUMATRA ISLAND, ACEH, INDONESIA**

Senior MSS Officer Su Chin crouched as he ran from under the rotor arc careful to not be decapitated. A black Toyota Land Cruiser waited for him. As Su sat down in the front seat, the driver, Officer Tao Zhen, said, "Sir, twelve additional officers are deployed along the West Trans Sumatra Highway in four vehicles in the cities Blang Pidie, Tanjongbunga, here in Labuhanhaji, and Manggeng. The People's Navy is patrolling off the coast."

"Very good, Tao. Take us to the center of the operating area," Officer Su ordered, "I want to be close by when we catch these criminals."

***

Jon staggered out of the jungle with Angie on his shoulders. "Angie, there's a house a hundred meters down the hill. Hang on, brother, we're almost home," he said as he trudged down the slope. Angie moaned softly in acknowledgment. He was deteriorating with every passing second. Several minutes later, Jon stopped behind an old wooden shed and lowered Angie to the ground. The house sat by itself at the end of a long winding one-lane dirt road. He didn't see any electric poles but there was a new satellite dish on the rusting corrugated roof. A mild breeze was blowing away from him, but he could hear the faint hum of a generator. Jon leaned over close to his ear and said, "Angie, are you with me?"

"You're not going to kiss me, are you, mate?" Angie said as his laugh became a coughing fit.

Jon released a little water from his drinking tube to clean the tip before giving it to Angie. Angie had run out of water over an hour earlier. Jon felt around in Angie's pockets for more fentanyl but came up empty. He retrieved his ketamine from his IFAK and gave Angie an injection. "This should kick in soon, brother." Jon looked at the burn pile behind the shed. Amongst the ashes, he saw partially burned containers for acetone, anhydrous ammonia, red phosphorous, and hydrochloric and sulfuric acid. He turned back to Angie and said, "I think we stumbled across a meth lab. Keep your rifle ready. I'm going to go recon the house." Jon pointed his rifle around the corner of the shed. He observed the house through his ACOG 4×32 scope. "I don't see any guards outside or surveillance cameras. There's a Land Cruiser out front. I'll be back in a few minutes."

"It's cool. Take your time, mate," Angie replied with a smile. He had crossed over from agony to utter contentment in seconds.

Jon scanned the area one more time before he sprinted to a decrepit old tractor twenty meters closer to the side of the house. He went to one knee and took a quick peek around the large rear tire. The portable generator was ten meters behind the back door and was inside a shelter about the size of a large doghouse. It had a roof and three walls to protect the generator from the rain and deflect the noise away from the house.

It must be in the low eighties with 100% humidity, but all of the windows and doors are closed. There must be an air conditioner on the other side of the house. Maybe two cooks for the meth and three others for security. If they're smart, they'll have a sentry parked a mile or so down the road to warn them if the cops or military come, Jon thought.

He hurriedly made his way around the house and took cover behind a large teak tree twenty meters from the air conditioner. He fired one well aim shot into it from his suppressed HK416 rifle. He waited five minutes, but nothing happened. Frustrated, he fired five more into it. Shortly, a thin shirtless man walked around the corner with an old AK-47 rifle in his hands. He stopped and looked around for a moment before walking over to the A/C unit. He bent over to check the unit and upon seeing the holes, sprang to his feet and looked in

Jon's direction. Jon shot him in the chest before he could run.

One down four to go, Jon thought as he ran toward the back door. *Please, be unlocked. Please, be unlocked,* Jon grabbed the doorknob. Locked. *Dammit!* It looked to be a sturdy door made from teak or mahogany. *No way I'm kicking this thing open.* He stepped aside and politely but firmly knocked on the door. Seconds later another shirtless man with a full-face respirator opened the door. He was shouting something in rapid-fire Indonesian over his shoulder before he stopped mid-sentence upon seeing Jon's rifle.

Jon held his left index finger up in front of his lips in the international don't make a fucking sound signal and used his suppressor to push the man back into the room. Jon pulled the respirator off of the man's bald head and pulled it over his own. He spun Mr. Clean around, put his left hand on his shoulder, and pushed him toward the next room with his rifle in his back. Jon stopped Mr. Clean in the doorway and pushed him down on his knees. Upon seeing two cooks working at the table and one security man sitting on a chair with an AK across his lap watching soccer on TV, he shouted, "Hands on your heads, motherfuckers!" *If they didn't understand English and a rifle being pointed at them as the international signal to get your fucking hands up, well that was on them,* he thought.

The soccer fan immediately reached for his rifle and Jon shot him twice in the chest knocking him off his chair. Mr. Clean took this opportunity to drive his head back into Jon's groin. Jon doubled over and collapsed to the floor on his back. His legs wouldn't obey commands, but his arms did. Mr. Clean was on his feet, turning to attack Jon when Jon brought his rifle up and shot him three times. Jon moved his barrel to the cooks, but they remained standing at the table with their hands up.

"Do you speak English?" Jon asked between gasps.

They both nodded yes.

"If you move, I'll shoot you. Do you understand?" Jon asked.

"We understand," one of the cooks said.

Jon slowly got to his feet and stepped over Mr. Clean. He walked over to dead-check the soccer fan and picked up his AK. He dropped the magazine and ejected the round in the chamber before set-ting the rifle down on the chair. Jon quickly flex-cuffed the cooks and locked them in a bedroom. He found the Land Cruiser's keys in Mr. Clean's pocket. He hurried outside and started the Land Cruiser after moving the right seat back about six inches. He pulled up next to the shed and shouted, "Hey, Angie, let's go. I got us a ride."

Jon got Angie up on his good left leg and helped him hop to the back seat on the driver's side. Jon ran around to the passenger's side and pulled Angie inside, so his broken right leg rested on the driver's side rear seat. Jon jumped back in and sped off for the main road. He had already programmed the pick-up point into his ATAK-MIL tablet. He checked the fuel gauge, half a tank.

A couple of minutes later Jon turned right onto the main road and headed North. He didn't see any street signs but even if he had, he wouldn't have been able to read them. "Angie, this SUV is set up for off-roading. It has a push bumper, a roll bar, and a skid plate. Keep an eye on our six just in case any of the ChiComs spot us. These tinted windows should help some," Jon said. *I might have to try one of these out when I get home,* he thought. "I'm going to call Starlord," Jon said. Jon keyed the PTT on his secure radio, "Starlord, this is Streetwalker, over."

"Go for Starlord."

"Starlord, barring any complications, Streetwalker ETA fifteen mikes," Jon transmitted.

"Starlord copies."

***

"Officer Su, this is Officer Fu Lian," Fu transmitted over the radio.

"Yes, report, Fu," Su replied.

"Sir, a white Land Cruiser just turned off of Sarina Jaya Road onto West Trans Sumatra Highway and drove away at high speed to the North," Fu said.

"Were the occupants Caucasian?" Su asked.

"Unknown, sir, the windows are tinted," Fu replied.

"Excellent, Fu. All cars to the North prepare an ambush on the highway in the farmland North of the village. We want the Americans alive if possible. They must not escape," Su transmitted. He shouted to his driver, "Turn South! Hurry!"

***

It was only ten miles from the drug lab to the pickup point but traffic on the two-lane highway was moving between thirty and forty miles per hour. "How are you doing, Angie? Don't fall asleep on me," Jon said as he glanced back in the rearview mirror.

"I'm still with you, Jonnie. Thanks for the ketamine. I'm feeling no pain right now," Angie smiled at Jon.

"Well, we'll be at—look out!" Jon shouted just before a black Nissan Pathfinder slammed into their right side, breaking his side mirror and pushing the Land Cruiser halfway off the pavement. Jon looked at the occupants and saw two armed Chinese men looking back. He could see them, but they couldn't see him through his tinted windows. "Hang on Angie!" Jon shouted as he steered back onto the pavement and slowed enough to bring his right front fender parallel with the Pathfinder's left rear fender. He jerked his front wheels to the right and slammed into the Pathfinder's left rear fender causing the Pathfinder's rear to rotate to the right off the pavement. Jon accelerated, pushing the Pathfinder perpendicular to the roadway. The Pathfinder's right rear tire caught on a small depression in the dirt causing the Pathfinder to flip up into the air and tumble down the highway. A man flew from the open left window and landed on the pavement only to be crushed by the Pathfinder as it continued to roll. Jon dodged around the SUV and accelerated away. He swerved in and out of his lane honking his horn before he turned off the highway at the next residential street, hoping no other MSS officers saw the PIT maneuver on the Pathfinder.

"Jon, a red Honda Pilot just turned down the road behind us. He's coming up fast," Angie yelled from the backseat.

Jon checked his rearview mirror and shouted back, "Roger, I see him! Hang on!" He turned hard right at the next intersection to continue North toward the pick-up point.

***

"Officer Fu! Report!" Senior Officer Su transmitted over the radio. He estimated he was still several minutes away. He was trying to follow the action by listening to the radio and watching the map on his GPS. "Fu! Report!" he transmitted again.

"Officer Su, this is Officer Hui Jing. Officer Fu is dead. The American flipped Fu's vehicle over. We are now following the Americans through residential streets. They are heading toward the farmland South of Blang Pidie. We are in pursuit," Officer Hui replied.

"Well done, Officer Hui. I will no longer allow good men to die. Deadly force is authorized. They must not escape. They must pay for their crimes against the People. I will intercept them from the North," Officer Su transmitted.

***

"Jon, that red Honda—Crikey!" Angie shouted as he scrunched down behind his seat to avoid the bullets that shattered the rear window. Several spidered the windshield to Jon's left causing him to flinch and involuntarily swerve to the right. "I got this, mate!" Angie shouted as he raised his Colt M4 over the seat back with his right hand and rested the barrel on top of a stack of ammonium nitrate fertilizer bags. "Hit the brakes, Jon!" he shouted. Jon slammed on the pedal and quickly slowed to a stop as the Honda shuttered to a stop a mere twenty feet behind them. Angie took careful aim at the passenger armed with the machine gun and poured half a mag into him before giving the driver the other half. Jon accelerated away through the crowded narrow residential road. He slammed on the brakes again, this time to avoid a kid chasing a soccer ball. "Shit!" he shouted, "We can't just blow through here like we did on the highway."

"Streetwalker, Starlord, over," he transmitted.

"Go for Streetwalker," Jon replied.

"I'm about to land at the PZ. What's your ETA?" Starlord asked.

Jon glanced at his ATAK tablet attached to his chest rig and transmitted, "Two mikes, over."

"Copy, two mikes, out," Starlord confirmed.

***

As Starlord flew over the pick-up point a mere 300 feet above the ground in his Cessna U206 just under its never exceed speed he pulled the throttle back to idle and wrapped the plane up into a 60° angle of bank descending and decelerating left turn. His landing gear was fixed so there was no need to extend them. Pulling two Gs in the turn he went to full flaps as he passed abeam the landing point at 200 feet. He continued his speed bleeding turn until he was over the road. He leveled his wings and just above stall speed, drove the plane onto the ad hoc runway in typical controlled crash Navy fashion. *Flare to land, squat to pee,* he thought. He braked to a stop and looked into the distance. *Plenty of room for takeoff even with three men aboard,* he thought. He punched the instrument panel clock's timer before turning in his seat. He reached back and brought his Minimi forward. The Minimi was a short-barreled M249 Squad Automatic Weapon with a collapsible stock. He had an ACOG scope and three 200-round box magazines.

Starlord set the brake and jumped out of the cockpit. He ran around to the cargo door on the right side. He released the tie-downs and quick disconnects before dragging the empty collapsible auxiliary fuel tank out of the plane and dropping it on the road. He dragged it to the side of the road and jumped back into the cockpit. He scanned the area in front and behind his plane with his binoculars. He picked this road because it was long and secluded with farmland on both sides. He could see for at least a mile in all directions. Danger could only come from the road. He hoped Streetwalker would be on time. He checked the clock. He looked up and saw three SUVs turn onto the road and drive toward him. They stopped about 700 meters away.

"Starlord! We see you! We're coming up on your tail, now!" Jon transmitted.

"Roger. I've got company. Three SUVs stopped about 700 meters off my nose. I think they're waiting until I takeoff," Starlord replied.

Jon slid to a stop on the hard-packed dirt and loose gravel. "We're here, Angie," he said as he hopped out and quickly carried Angie over to the Cessna. The overhead fiberglass cargo door had already been raised. Jon laid Angie inside and pushed him across the floor. Jon got in on his knees and looked over Starlord's shoulder.

"What do you think?" Starlord asked.

"I think they are more fucking MSS bastards and they're going to shoot us down as soon as we takeoff. They shot down Angie's Black Hawk with a MANPAD. Give me your Minimi. I'll take care of them. Just turn out to the left and stay below 100 feet," Jon said.

"Okay, here we go," Starlord said as he held the brakes while fire-walling the throttle. When the engine was at max performance, he let off the brakes, and the little plane lunged forward. Jon clipped the Minimi to his chest rig and put his clear eye pro on. He lay out on the floor with his head sticking out of the cargo door at floor level. Angie rolled over on top of Jon's lower body to keep him from falling out. Jon could see the first SUV in the distance as soon as Starlord raised the nose gear off the road. After 950 feet the Cessna lifted off and Starlord accelerated toward the SUVs at 50 feet. 500 feet from them, he banked left giving Jon a perfect view of the threat from only 150 meters. Jon brought the Minimi to his shoulder and took aim through the ACOG.

***

"Conceal yourselves behind my vehicle until the airplane is in the air then fire everything we have at him as he flies over us," Senior Officer Su Chin said to his men. Two of them had QW-3 shoulder-launched surface-to-air missiles. The other four carried Norinco QBZ-95 bullpup assault rifles. Su smiled, believing the little unarmed airplane didn't stand a chance. The plane took off and accelerated right at him. He was giddy with excitement. He had been physically unfit for military service.

This would be his only opportunity to command fighting men in the field.

"Sir, he is turning away!" Officer Hui shouted.

"No! Fire the missiles!" he ordered as he turned to Hui.

"The airplane is too low for the missiles to acquire its heat signature. They won't launch until it climbs," Hui replied.

Senior Officer Su Chin turned to look at the little unarmed Cessna in time to see a long hose of red tracer rounds zip toward him, but he didn't have time to scream as a devastating torrent of hate riddled his vehicles and men. The vehicles burned and the men bled out. The two hundred rounds in the magazine were enough to annihilate his small command in less than ten seconds.

***

"Target destroyed," Jon transmitted calmly before scooting back inside the plane and pulling the cargo area's overhead door down. Starlord climbed away leaving behind three burning SUVs and a bloody mess. Black smoke billowed above the scene signaling where to send the Blang Pidie Street Department for clean up.

"Hey, mate. Do you know what time it is? It's beer o'clock," Angie said before laughing at his own joke.

"Sorry, brother. I think we'll have to wait," Jon replied.

"Check my emergency cooler back there in the tail," Starlord said.

Jon leaned back, grabbed the blue plastic cooler, and pulled it to him. He moved the ice around and said, "It looks like you have a choice between water, Blue Gatorade, or Victoria Bitter."

"Outstanding, mate! Give me the VB. Starlord, you are obviously a man of discerning taste," Angie said.

CHAPTER 10

1300, JULY 21, DAY 7,
BASE HOSPITAL,
PAYA LEBAR AIR BASE, SINGAPORE

"I hope you're decent, brother. I'm coming in," Jon said as he pushed the curtain aside. He stepped up to the side of Angie's bed. "You look a lot better when you're cleaned up and not all covered in leeches," Jon said with a smile. Angie's left arm was in a cast, and he wore a sling to immobilize his shoulder. The cast on his right leg went from his right foot to above his knee.

"Back at you, mate," Angie said.

Jon shrugged his backpack off and sat it on the edge of the bed. He unzipped the top and stuck his hand inside. "You still like Foster's, right?" Jon asked, knowing the answer.

"Fuck no! I don't drink that horse piss!" He shot back.

Jon smiled and pulled a cold bottle of Victoria Bitter from his pack. He twisted off the top and put it in Angie's left hand. Angie tried to raise it to his mouth but winced in pain and gave up, switching it to his right hand. "Prick!" Angie said before he took a long pull on the bottle.

Jon grinned and took a drink from his own. "I'll hide the rest of these in your bedside table before I leave," he said. Jon pulled a red Sharpie out of his pocket and asked, "Hey, can I sign your cast?"

"Well, considering you did save my life, sure, but no cock and balls shit," Angie replied.

Jon started writing down on Angie's leg cast where it was hard for him to see. "Scout's honor. So, what's your prognosis?" Jon asked.

"Our Doc says, six to nine months of rehab to get my shoulder back to 100%," Angie replied. "What's next for you?" Angie asked.

"My swim buddy, Clint, got me a position on his SOG team. We're going to work up for a few months and then deploy to Iraq and Syria," Jon replied.

Angie finished his bottle and motioned for another. "One of my mates told me JSOC's local det commander, Brigadier General Edward Sanford, is here in the hospital with a broken nose and two broken arms. The general's arms will be in casts for at least six weeks. My mate said someone called 999 for him. He was found unconscious at the bottom of the stairs in his apartment. He was naked except for sparkling red lipstick and a matching red bra and panties set."

Jon vigorously shook his head and said, "That's bullshit. The bra and panties were white. You know that see-through lacy stuff."

Angie laughed and then winced in pain. "You're flying too close to the Sun, mate. He may send some of his D-boys after you."

"Naw, they know he's a dumb ass. Besides, they like me better than him," Jon replied.

A smiling little Singaporean Air Force nurse came around the curtain and saw the beer bottles.

She frowned immediately and took the bottles away from them and turned them upside down in the sink to drain. She turned to Jon and said, "It is time for Mr. Hawkins's sponge bath."

"That's okay. I don't mind if he doesn't," Jon replied.

"Go," she said as she put her tiny hand against Jon's chest and pushed him past the curtain and out of the room.

"I'll catch you later, Angie," Jon said from the hall before leaving.

Angie smiled as he shook his head. He was actually looking forward to the sponge bath. Then he remembered. "Miss, would you read what is written on my leg cast?"

She walked around the bed and looked down at his cast. "It says, me so horny. Me love you long time. XO XO XO, Sandy. She must love you very much."

Angie laughed and mumbled to himself, "Bastard!"

THE END

Please join my newsletter using the link below for updates on future Jon Smith novels and short stories. I promise I won't sell or share your email address with others.

Bob Asher Books Newsletter

ABOUT THE AUTHOR

Bob is a retired supervisory intelligence officer with the National Geospatial-Intelligence Agency (NGA). He grew up in and around St. Louis, Missouri. By the time he was in high school he knew he wanted to do two things with his life: fly in the military and work in law enforcement. After graduating from Parks College of St. Louis University with a degree in Aeronautics he earned a commission in the USMC. He became a Naval Aviator flying the CH-53D Sea Stallion helicopter. After his active duty, he returned to the St. Louis area and worked as a police officer. When the Twin Towers were attacked, he joined the Missouri Army National Guard and flew Black Hawk helicopters in Iraq during Operation Iraqi Freedom II. While in Iraq he applied for and accepted a position with NGA. Now he and his wife live a quiet life in the country surrounded by trees.